Devils' Pass is published by Stone Arch Books, a Capstone Imprint
1710 Roe Crest Drive
North Mankato, Minnesota 56003
www.mycapstone.com

Library of Congress Cataloging-in-Publication Data is available on the Library of
Congress website.

ISBN: 978-1-4965-4988-4 (hardcover)
ISBN: 978-1-4965-4992-1 (ebook pdf)

Summary: Evie Allen must use her wicked smart brains to figure out whether or
not there is a zombie infestation — and figure out who the zombies are and most
importantly, how to defeat them.

Editor: Megan Atwood
Designer: Hilary Wacholz

Printed and bound in
010382F17

DEVILS' PASS

EVIE ALLEN
VS.
THE QUIZ BOWL ZOMBIES

BY JUSTINA IRELAND
ILLUSTRATED BY TYLER CHAMPION

STONE ARCH BOOKS
a capstone imprint

THE LOYAL ORDER OF HELGA

Long, long ago, in a village called New Svalbard, the people who lived there faced unimaginable dangers. A sinkhole as old as time held a door – a portal – to the Otherside, a dark and dreadful place filled with literal nightmares.

To warn travelers of the danger the village posed, the people renamed it Devils' Pass – a reminder to all who lived there and passed through that a darkness sat in the area. A darkness that often had teeth.

For years the people of Devils' Pass endured the danger. Then Helga, one of the white settlers of the village, fell through the cursed sinkhole to the Otherside, coming face-to-face with the terrifying monsters. Helga spent many years there, fighting all sorts of monstrous creatures, learning about their ways and their weaknesses. Through trials and tribulations, and more than a little cunning, she became a fearsome warrior.

Helga fought her way back to Devils' Pass through the portal, now with an understanding of the deadly secrets of the Otherside. Almost immediately, her skills were put to the test. A fearsome frost giant menaced the village, crawling out of the sinkhole and terrorizing the people. Using only a flaming torch, Helga fought the giant and won. It was an astonishing act of bravery – but soon it was clear that the people of Devils' Pass suffered from something else. The sinkhole made the people of the village forget that monsters lived there.

Through some type of magic, however, not all of them forgot. Those who remembered the perils and nightmares the sinkhole brought forth became the Loyal Order of Helga. Along with Helga, the people who remembered the danger vowed to protect Devils' Pass – and the entire world – from the vicious monsters of the Otherside.

CHAPTER ONE
Show Them What You've Got

"In your homework last night, we discussed the scientific method. Can anyone come to the board and outline what it is?" Mrs. Fillman looked out across the room, searching for a victim. All the kids slouched down in their seats a little, hoping she wouldn't see them.

That is, everyone except Evie Allen, who sat up straighter and raised her hand. "I know," she called, waving her hand in the air.

"Anyone but Evie," Ms. Fillman said. The students were quick to look down at their books or notebooks to avoid Ms. Fillman's searching gaze.

Evie sighed. "Can I please just answer the question, Ms. Fillman?"

Ms. Fillman nodded, and Evie beamed. This was her favorite part of science class, answering questions on the board. She just couldn't figure out why no one else wanted to do it.

Evie walked to the board, hopping over the backpacks in the aisle and ignoring the kids who whispered as she passed. She was used to it. Skipping a grade meant that she was smaller than everyone else, and everyone in eighth grade at Devils' Pass Middle School knew her as the really smart girl who answered all the questions in almost every class.

Evie picked up one of the dry erase markers, the orange one, and began to work through the problem on the whiteboard. When she was done, she capped the marker and put it back in the tray.

"Good job, Evie. As usual," Ms. Fillman said.

The bell rang, and people packed up their books and notebooks. "Your homework is on the board. Make sure to do the even questions only! And study for the test this Friday," Ms Fillman called as everyone filed out of the room.

Evie went back to her desk and packed up her stuff. She threw her book bag over her shoulder and started to leave, but Ms. Fillman stopped her before she walked out the door.

"Evie, may I have a word with you?" she called.

Evie walked over to Ms. Fillman's desk. Ms. Fillman took off her glasses and wiped them on the corner of her cardigan. "Evie, I know you like answering the questions on the board, but you need to give the rest of the class a chance to participate."

"Oh, OK," Evie said. It hadn't occurred to her that volunteering to answer every question meant that she was taking an opportunity away from someone else. After all, no one else wanted to answer the questions.

"You're very smart, Evie. But I worry that maybe you're too focused on school. Tell me, do you have any activities outside of your schoolwork?" Ms. Fillman asked.

Evie shifted from foot to foot. She and her friends, the Loyal Order of Helga, did spend their time hunting down and destroying the monsters that threatened Devils' Pass, but she couldn't very well tell Ms. Fillman that. "Um, I like to read about stuff. I like science."

Ms. Fillman gave Evie a polite smile. "That's what I thought. I think you work very hard, Evie, but I also think engaging with the real world every once in a while will help you get some balance in your life."

Evie did engage in the real world. But somehow she thought telling Ms. Fillman about saving the town from cookie elves wouldn't help her plead her case.

Ms. Fillman went on. "I have an idea. Perhaps you could put your mind to good use and socialize while you're at it. This could help you branch out."

Ms. Fillman reached into her desk and pulled out a pink flyer. On the front was the headline "Do you think you're smart?" and a picture of a woman with a cloud of question marks around her head.

"The high school is hosting a quiz show for ages thirteen to seventeen and they're having tryouts all this week after school. I think it might be a good outlet for your, er, energy. Plus, think of how much fun it would be to be on TV. And of all the people you'd get to meet. Plus, if you get on the show, you're guaranteed to win at least five hundred dollars!"

Evie took the flyer. There were several dates for tryouts and one of them was today. "Oh, this looks cool! Thanks, Ms. Fillman."

Evie left and headed to her next class, the flyer gripped in her hand. Maybe she did spend too much time poring over her schoolwork. This could be a good way to do something that 1) wasn't school related, 2) let her use her brains, and 3) wouldn't put her in mortal danger.

Ms. Fillman was right. This quiz show was perfect for her.

CHAPTER TWO
Buck Up for the Bucks

Over lunch Evie shared the flyer with her friends. They had mixed reactions.

"That looks hard," Zach Lopez said, pushing his floppy brown hair out of his eyes. Zach was originally from L.A. and had only moved to Devils' Pass recently. He'd quickly managed to fit in even though he was one of the few brown people in town.

Zach's mom was the principal of Devils' Pass Middle School, so that helped some. But he mostly fit in because he was a member of the Loyal Order of Helga just like Evie and the rest of her friends. As members of the LOH — the only members, in fact — they were tasked with fighting the monsters that tried to eat the people in town. Monsters that were always up to something sinister.

"I think it looks awesome," Tiffany Donovan said, finishing the last of the tuna casserole off her tray. Tiffany was Evie's favorite person at Devils' Pass Middle School. At nearly six feet tall with poofy hair and dark skin, it was hard to miss Tiffany. She was also the bravest person Evie knew. Even when Evie wasn't feeling bold, Tiffany was always willing to face down danger. Which was important in a town that was always getting attacked by monsters.

"I could see you and Tiffany doing this, Ev, but I can't imagine I'd be any good. I barely got a C on my last math test," said Jeff, Evie's older brother. Jeff had pale skin just like Evie, but while her hair was brown, his was blond and he wore glasses. Jeff was a cancer survivor and his left leg had been amputated in a procedure known as rotationplasty. His foot had been reattached at his knee to allow him to more easily wear a prosthesis, but Jeff was still uncomfortable with the prosthetic leg and only wore it sometimes. Today, he had his crutches, his pant leg rolled up and safety pinned.

"I don't know, I think it might be fun," Evie said, looking at the flyer once more.

"I think we should all go try out. You never know what they're looking for. Plus, there's a five hundred dollar cash prize if you make it on the show. That's pretty sweet," Tiffany said. She pointed at the nearly untouched pile of tuna casserole on Jeff's tray. "Are you going to eat that?"

Jeff slid his tray across the table at Tiffany, his nose wrinkled in disgust. "I don't know how you eat that stuff," he said.

"It's delicious," Tiffany said, her mouth full.

"Tiffany is right, we should try out. You never know what will happen," Zach said. "Speaking of which, did you see the story on the news about the people who drove into the lake over in Sylverna?"

Evie shook her head. "Sylverna is like ten miles away. When did this happen?"

"Yesterday. Mason Briggs was talking about it in science and he said the story wasn't going public because the police didn't know how to report it," Zach said, frowning.

"OK, but Mason is the guy who was convinced that eating that popping candy and drinking a soda would make your stomach literally explode," Tiffany pointed out.

"This story sounds like it's serious business, though. Jeff heard Mason's story too — we're in science class together," Zach said. Jeff nodded and Zach went on, "An entire family in their car, heads cracked open and their brains missing."

"What, like zombies?" squeaked Evie.

"This sounds too ordinary for Otherside monsters," said Tiffany. "I mean, if there were zombies from the Otherside, they'd have some kind of elaborate plan to get brains, not just trap people in a car, I bet. When have the monsters ever been that easy?"

Jeff nodded. "Exactly. The Otherside monsters have created apps and cookie cults just to try to eat people. This seems kind of straightforward. Plus, Mason did tell everyone last year that he'd taught his dog how to talk. I don't know that I believe his story."

"I think we should keep it in . . . mind," Zach said, a sly smile on his face.

Tiffany rolled her eyes. "Haha, very funny. Zombies, mind, hilarious."

"I agree with Zach," Evie said. "Maybe this time we could stop the monsters before anyone gets hurt. I mean, besides the family in Sylverna."

Jeff shrugged. "I have a free period in computer science today. I could look it up and see if it's true."

"Sounds good," Tiffany said, tapping the flyer for the quiz show. "I think we should try out. Five hundred dollars if we get on the show, more if we win. That's a lot of money."

"But we're going to be up against high school kids," Evie said.

Tiffany shrugged. "So? We can beat them. I'm way smarter than my sister. Besides, we've beaten evil mermaids, carnivorous unicorns, and vampires that learned how to program just so they could drink up people's souls. How hard can it be to beat a few high schoolers?"

CHAPTER THREE
Brainiacs Unite

Devils' Pass High School was on the opposite side of town from the middle school. The easiest way to get there was through the park, so after school Evie, Tiffany, Jeff, and a very reluctant Zach made their way down the path that bisected the park.

Devils' Pass Park was nice if you didn't think too hard about the monsters that came from the sinkhole in the back of it. People jogged on the path and there were a few folks walking their dogs, their heads tucked deep into their collars against the cold. There was a playground where little kids played, and the grass was a great place for a game of football or soccer.

But at the back of the park was a sinkhole filled with dark, inky water surrounded by a rusty chain-link fence that rattled like old bones when the wind blew. The water of the sinkhole hid a portal to a place known as the Otherside, a land of monsters that fed on regular people. Tons of monsters had come out of the portal, but not many people had been to the Otherside. The only person Evie knew who had managed to go to there and come back was Mr. Hofstrom, the town librarian. But something had happened to Mr. Hofstrom on the Otherside. It was the reason he lived at the library and couldn't or wouldn't leave it.

No one knew what that something was, though.

Evie and her friends hurried through the park. Even though it was early, it was overcast, the sky gray with a few snowflakes swirling around. The clouds made it darker than it should have been for the time of day and drew out the shadows in the park. Among the four of them, all conversation stopped as they rushed down the path. Evie wondered if they all felt the same foreboding she experienced every time she set foot in the park. It was a relief once they got past the sinkhole, the path depositing them in the neighborhood where Devils' Pass High School sat.

"Where are the quiz show tryouts being held?" Tiffany asked. She pulled an apple out of her coat pocket and bit into it noisily.

Evie pulled the crumpled flyer advertising the quiz show from her coat pocket. "It looks like the cafeteria. Do you know where that is?" she asked Tiffany. Tiffany had a sister in eleventh grade, and she was the only one of them who had been to the high school before.

"Yeah, it's toward the back of the school. Come on," she said, leading the way. Everyone followed.

"I really don't think this is a good idea. We should be investigating the zombies that ate that family's brains," Zach said.

"Oh, come on," said Tiffany. "You know that's

totally just Mason making up stories again. And anyway, that didn't even happen in Devils' Pass."

"I don't think Mason made it up," Jeff said. "I heard Melissa Stanton talking about it after lunch. Her dad is a police officer, and she said that she heard him discussing it with her mom over dinner. They think it might have been an animal attack of some kind."

"What kind of animal just eats brains?" Evie asked.

"No kind," Jeff said, adjusting his glasses. "That's why we should be checking it out."

Tiffany rolled her eyes. "What do you think, Evie?" she asked.

Evie shrugged. She wasn't good at picking sides in arguments, and she didn't like fighting. She needed more to time to think about it. She furrowed her eyebrows. "I don't know. It does seem kind of weird for zombies to just eat someone without any kind of trickery," she said. The boys crossed their arms, but she went on, "I mean, usually the monsters are a lot smarter."

"That is a good point," Zach said. "But I still think we should check it out."

"How about we go talk to Mr. Hofstrom at the library after the quiz show tryouts?" Evie offered. "He'd know better than anyone else what zombies are like."

"Or if they're even real," Tiffany said. She held her hand up to a door with a flyer taped to it. It was the same flyer as Evie held in her hand. "Ta-da! I present to you, the cafeteria. Now, let's go show everyone how smart we are."

CHAPTER FOUR

The Luckiest Kids

The Devils' Pass High School cafeteria looked like a larger version of the Devils' Pass Middle School cafeteria. There were rows and rows of tables and stainless steel cafeteria counters that looked like they had been wiped down and closed up hours ago. Along one wall there was also a line of vending machines with soda and snacks that the middle school didn't have. Zach pointed them out as they entered the room.

"No fair! How come we don't have vending machines?"

"Because middle schoolers cannot be trusted with the incredible power and responsibility of potato chips," Jeff said.

Evie looked around the cafeteria. There were a lot more people than she'd been expecting. Most of the kids sitting around looked older — definitely high schoolers — but there were a few kids that she recognized from the middle school.

"There are a lot of people here," Evie said. "Maybe we should go."

"No way! Five hundred bucks just to be chosen is a lot of bucks," Tiffany joked. "Come on, let's find a table."

As they headed to a table in the middle of the cafeteria, Evie overheard a group of girls talking at a table near the door. One of them, a familiar-looking girl with dark skin, gestured wildly with her hands. "Anyway, the story is when they dragged the car out of Foggy Bottom Lake, all of them were missing their brains."

"No. Way." A blond, pony-tailed girl wearing a red sweater leaned in close to the dark-skinned girl telling the story. "So, what happened to their brains? Was it like organ thieves or something?"

Tiffany stopped next to the table, and Evie stopped as well. Tiffany crossed her arms and turned to the table full of chattering girls. "Don't tell me you actually believe that?" The dark-skinned high school girl at the table grinned at Tiffany.

"What are you doing here, loser?" the girl said with a grin. Evie finally realized why the girl telling the story looked familiar: it was Tiffany's older sister, Simone. Evie had met Simone a couple of times, but not enough to remember what she looked like. But she should've realized the girl at the table was Tiffany's sister; the two of them looked almost exactly alike.

"Uh, obviously I'm here to win the five hundred dollars. And to be on television," Tiffany said.

Simone laughed. "Good luck with that." Simone patted her hair and turned her back to Tiffany, signaling the conversation was over.

Evie pulled on Tiffany's arm. "Come on, let's go sit with the boys. We'll show her. Winning is the best revenge."

Tiffany nodded and walked with Evie. "She's so going down," Tiffany said. "Look, there's an old guy. I'm going to ask him what we need to do to sign up." Tiffany headed to the front of the room in the direction of an older white man wearing a sweater vest over a white shirt. He had a stack of papers in front of him and handed them out to kids as they walked up.

Evie sat down at the table with Zach and Jeff. The boys were playing some kind of game with a folded-up triangle of paper, each taking turns holding up their hands like goalposts before the other person flicked the paper through the finger uprights. Evie sighed.

"Guys," Evie said, "Simone and her friends were talking about the people with the missing brains at the bottom of Foggy Bottom Lake."

Jeff flicked the paper triangle but it went wide of Zach's hands. "Really? That seems kind of weird."

"Why?" Zach asked.

"Because normal people don't usually know about the monsters. Goldfish memory, remember?" Jeff said. For some reason, people in the town never remembered any of the monsters that came from the sinkhole, a phenomenon Tiffany called goldfish memory. There were only a handful of people who remembered the monsters that attacked: the mayor, Mr. Hofstrom (the town librarian), and the Loyal Order of Helga, which consisted of Evie, Tiffany, Jeff, and Zach. It was a frustrating thing, since no matter how many times they saved the town, no one really seemed to know that they were heroes. But it was also kind of cool, because it meant that they could still lead normal lives.

Well, as normal a life as someone could have and still fight monsters.

"I think Tiffany is right," Evie said. "That story about the car in the lake has to be a hoax."

The boys exchanged a look, like Evie was being silly. But before they could say anything, a man standing in the front of the room leaned over and tapped on a microphone.

"Hello, can I get everyone's attention? Thank you," he said as folks quieted down. "My name is Hans Gehrin, and I am the coordinator for Super Quiz Show, a show all about brains!"

People clapped weakly. He went on. "I'm excited to meet all of you and to get to know your sweet, amazing brains. Please come up and get an interview sheet if you haven't already. Fill it out completely with your name, age, and favorite subject, and then answer the fun and easy questions. Best of luck!"

People crowded up to get the interview sheets as soon as the man was done talking.

"All right, so this looks pretty easy," Tiffany said, as she returned to the table and sat down next to Zach. She had four sheets of paper and four pencils. "All we have to do is fill out these forms."

Evie glanced down at the questions and frowned. "These questions are weird. 'How many cupcakes do you usually eat in a month?' What do cupcakes have to do with anything?"

Tiffany shrugged. "I don't know. Maybe they're just trying to figure out people's personalities?"

Zach frowned. "'Do you watch at least six hours of television a day?' OK, that's kind of personal," he said. "No one needs to know how much TV I watch every day."

"They aren't going to tell your mom," Evie said, laughing.

Jeff nodded. "Let's just answer these questions and get over to talk to Mr. Hofstrom."

"How do we know if we get to be on the show?" Evie asked.

Tiffany shrugged. "Maybe they'll tell us after we fill out the forms."

Everyone bent their heads over the forms and began to fill them out. Evie glanced at the questions once, quickly, before going through and answering each one. No wonder everyone in the cafeteria seemed so excited. The questions weren't about anything like science or math; they were mostly just about what kinds of foods everyone liked to eat.

Evie completed the form and took it to the front table, Tiffany right behind her. Jeff finished next, then Zach. By this point people were laughing and talking. They'd expected a hard, facts-based test and gotten questions about their favorite kind of pizza instead.

Zach grinned as he sat back down. "That was the easiest quiz, ever. If only school was like that!"

"It didn't seem weird to you that a quiz show wouldn't ask any questions about, I don't know, trivia?" Evie asked.

Zach shrugged. "Maybe it's like one of those quiz shows where you try to answer a question and have to do a wacky physical challenge if you get it wrong. I mean, there were a lot of food questions on there. Why else would they care about what we eat?"

Tiffany held up a glossy pamphlet. "This was sitting on the table next to the quizzes. It looks like this is for a brand new show, but I don't think it has any physical challenges." They bent around the pamphlet, which showed a fancy stage that looked like just a generic game show. There was a girl photographed mid-jump, clutching money in both her hands.

"What channel is this going to be on?" Evie asked.

Nobody knew. It didn't say anywhere on the pamphlet.

Mr. Gehrin stood up and called for everyone's attention. "Excuse me, excuse me. Could I have the following people come to the front for an additional interview: Mason Briggs, Shelby Brannigan, Adam Paul, and Gerald Bringham. I'm afraid those are the only folks we want to talk to tonight. Everyone else: please come back tomorrow for round two of our tryouts. Thank you, and have a good night."

The four people selected jumped up and down, their friends congratulating them as they made their way to where the older man waited for them.

"Mason Briggs? Really?" Tiffany shook her head in

disgust. "He is the luckiest guy alive."

Jeff cleared his throat. "Um, remember when his arm was eaten by cookie elves?"

Tiffany laughed. "OK, yeah . . . I guess I'm just mad I wasn't picked."

Evie sighed and patted Tiffany on the shoulder. "I'm disappointed, too. Don't be jealous. We can try again tomorrow. Come on, let's swing by the library and see what Mr. Hofstrom knows about monsters that eat brains."

Tiffany nodded, but she was still pouting. Neither Jeff nor Zach seemed upset at not being chosen. They were clearly just there because it was something to do.

But Evie understood how Tiffany felt. She was disappointed — really disappointed. Why hadn't she been selected? And why weren't the questions harder, trivia-type questions? Evie wasn't good at a lot of things, but she was good at being smart. And the one time when she thought that was going to be useful and help her win a prize, it hadn't.

Evie watched as the four people selected to go with the old man followed him down a hallway and sighed. She rested her chin on her hand.

There went the four luckiest kids in Devils' Pass.

CHAPTER FIVE

The Toughest Monsters

It was late by the time they left the high school cafeteria, and everyone was hungry. Rather than go to the library and talk to Mr. Hofstrom right away, everyone decided to wait until the next morning to seek him out.

"We still don't know if it's a real thing or just a rumor," Jeff said. "Let's wait until tomorrow to talk to Mr. Hofstrom."

They all agreed and went home, so the next morning Zach, Tiffany, Evie, and Jeff arrived at the library bright and early. Tiffany pressed the buzzer and applied the code of long-long-short-short pushes that let Mr. Hofstrom know there was Loyal Order of Helga business.

Mr. Hofstrom appeared at the door a few minutes later, yawning widely. "Morning, yo. What's up?" Mr. Hofstrom looked much younger than he was, and he talked a little like an old movie from the eighties. He also dressed in tracksuits and running shoes, his skin dark against the red lapel of his track jacket. Evie always thought he looked like one of the rappers on the old CDs her dad liked to listen to, what he called "Classic Hip Hop."

"Good morning, Mr. Hofstrom," Tiffany said. "Can you tell us what you know about monsters that eat brains?"

"You mean like zombies?" Mr. Hofstrom drank from his mug.

Zach's face went pale. "Zombies are real?"

Mr. Hofstrom nodded. "Yep. And they're some straight nasty. Probably the scariest of the Otherside monsters. Come on in. Anyone want hot cocoa?"

Everyone nodded and followed Mr. Hofstrom into the library.

Outside, the Devils' Pass Library was an old-fashioned building with columns and steps that made the building look imposing and very serious, like important learning was happening inside. But the inside of the building was warm and welcoming, with colorful posters and lots of books. The town library was one of Evie's favorite places.

They followed Mr. Hofstrom past the public computer bank and the stacks of books to a door that was marked EMPLOYEES ONLY. In that room was a sort of kitchen with a table where everyone could sit comfortably. Because Mr. Hofstrom didn't leave the library, he had to have a place to sit and make food, and that room was it. There was also a desk in one corner where Mr. Hofstrom usually sat, but today he went to the electric kettle and used it to pour hot water into four cups filled with hot cocoa powder. After he stirred them all, he handed each of the kids a mug and everyone settled in.

"So, what's the deal with the zombies? What do you know?" Mr. Hofstrom asked.

Very quickly, Tiffany and Jeff filled him in on the rumor floating around about the family found at the bottom of Foggy Bottom Lake with missing brains.

Mr. Hofstrom sipped his hot cocoa. "That doesn't sound clever enough for Otherside monsters. They're usually more careful in how they trap people."

"That's what I thought," Tiffany said, looking pointedly at Jeff and Zach.

"But we can't dismiss anything. You never know when one of these monsters is going to attack the town, or how." Mr. Hofstrom went to his desk and pulled out the Trapper Keeper, a plastic notebook, where he kept all of his monster information.

He flipped through a few pages while Evie and the others sipped their cocoa and looked on.

"Here we are," Mr. Hofstrom said, landing on the page in the notebook that he'd been looking for. "Zombies. It looks like there are several different kinds of zombies. Not all zombies feed on brains. Some feed on livers, some on hearts."

"Gross," Zach said. He set down his cocoa and leaned back, looking a little ill.

"Zombies are definitely gross. But they're also smart. Smarter than vampires even. They should never be underestimated. This could be be the toughest monster you've ever faced," Mr. Hofstrom said.

"Oh, man," said Jeff. They'd faced down some vampires before and it had been a difficult fight.

"But how do we recognize them?" Evie asked. She didn't like having to fight monsters — she didn't like fighting anyone. But if she could recognize what the monsters looked like, she could maybe help her friends fight them.

"Can't we just tell by looking at them? I mean, they are zombies, after all. You might be overthinking it, Evie," Jeff said, smiling at her. But Evie frowned. She didn't think that was possible.

"Not necessarily," Mr. Hofstrom said, looking at the page in front of him. "It says here that zombies usually appear as kind folk, like teachers and coaches. They're very devoted to knowledge, and they love reading books and working on complicated projects. They wait until their prey isn't expecting the attack to strike. Oh, and their saliva has a narcotic effect."

Zach frowned. "They drug people?"

Mr. Hofstrom nodded. "Their saliva knocks people out. Kind of like a snake's venom. So even if people are being eaten, they stop fighting pretty quickly."

"How do we defeat them?" Tiffany asked.

Mr. Hofstrom shook his head. "No idea. It doesn't say in here."

"Wait, are you saying you don't know how to beat the zombies?" Zach asked.

"We don't even know if there are zombies here," Evie pointed out.

"That's right," Mr. Hofstrom said. "But that becomes the issue. First, we have to figure out whether or not there are zombies in town. Then, we have to find the thing that will beat them."

"That seems impossible," Jeff said, his shoulders slumping.

"Maybe, maybe not," Evie said. "We've been fighting monsters for a while. We can use the scientific method and use what other monsters are weak against." She settled in, excited to be on firm ground. "First," she said, "we come up with a hypothesis based on our other findings. Then, we test it out. If it works, we have a solution. If it doesn't, we change one of the variables — in this case, the monster killing method we've previously used — and we try again. Maybe something that has worked on other monsters will work against the zombies."

"If there even are zombies in town," Tiffany said. "That's our first step. Thanks for the hot cocoa,

Mr. Hofstrom." She stood up and put on her backpack. "Come on, guys. We don't want to be late for school."

"Good luck," Mr. Hofstrom said. "Remember, if there are zombies, strange things will start happening. But they'll be subtle. People may lose time, or end up in places they weren't expecting. People may disappear for a while, but then come back. They may be missing important body parts with no memory of how anything happened or even how they got hurt. Have you ever heard the story of the man who goes on vacation and wakes up in his hotel room in a bathtub full of ice? And finds out he's missing a kidney? Or the lady who goes in for eye surgery and wakes up without any eyeballs? Those are both true stories about zombies. That's how you'll find them. Look for strange patterns."

Evie put on her backpack and made her way to the door.

Mr. Hofstrom usually made her feel better about monster problems. But today, she felt even more freaked out than she had before they'd gone to visit him. With every other monster, the path was always straight forward. They found out what the monster's weakness was, and they used that to defeat it.

But now, for the first time ever, they didn't have the answer.

Luckily, Evie had a scientific mind. She would just have to use her brain to figure out what was going on.

CHAPTER SIX

Going with the Flow

The school cafeteria was abuzz with talk of the quiz show. After people learned about Mason Briggs getting picked and winning five hundred dollars, everyone decided that trying out for the quiz show was a great idea.

"I still cannot believe they picked Mason Briggs," Tiffany said. Evie felt the same way, but she didn't want to sound like a jerk. It was true, though — Mason was a nice guy, but he wasn't very smart. After all, he had told everyone at school how his cousin won a contest to go into space on a Russian space shuttle. Evie knew the launch schedule for the International Space Station by heart, and there was no way that his cousin had gotten to go there. Not only that, Mason told everyone his cousin was going to Mars after the stint at the Space Station. Evie knew from a book she had on the Mars Rover that it took almost a year to get to Mars, but Mason was convinced that his cousin had completed the entire trip over spring break. Everyone had heard that story and knew it wasn't true. But not Mason. He believed it until someone printed out a story talking about humans visiting Mars, making it clear that no such thing had ever happened.

"They must have been looking for something besides just being super smart," Jeff said. "Mason is a really good storyteller. Maybe that's why they picked him."

Tiffany rolled her eyes and took a big bite out of her taco. Evie poked at her vegetarian noodle salad. Why hadn't they picked her? She sighed. "I bet I didn't get picked because I'm just a boring nerd," Evie said, feeling a little sorry for herself. The conversation with

Ms. Fillman echoed in her mind. Maybe she should stop concentrating on school and being smart.

"What? No way," Tiffany said. "Remember that time you built that model plane out of popsicle sticks and rubber bands? It actually flew. That was super cool."

"Yeah, and also: no way are any of us boring," Jeff said. "We fight monsters."

"Even if nobody ever remembers it," said Tiffany.

Evie nodded, feeling a little better. "Are you guys planning on going back this evening to try again?"

"I can't," Tiffany said. "I have a field hockey clinic I have to go to. Field hockey tryouts are only three months away."

Zach walked up to the table and sat down, pulling a sandwich out of the brown bag he carried. "Are we talking about the quiz show?" he asked.

Evie nodded. "Yep. Are you going to try out again?"

"Um, I think I'm good. I really just went for moral support," he said with a laugh.

"Ditto," said Jeff. "Plus I have to get started on a paper. It's due in a week."

"I can walk with you to the tryouts after school, Evie," Tiffany said. "My field hockey clinic is in the high school gym."

"Okay. So what should we do about the zombies?" Evie asked.

"We don't even know if there are zombies. The more I think about it, the more it seems like just one of Mason's stories," Zach said.

Evie shook her head. "Maybe. But it seems strange so many people are repeating the same story. I guess we could just ask Mason Briggs, since he's the first person we know who told it. Maybe he knows something that could help."

"He wasn't in class today," Jeff said. "I think he's sick."

"Well, maybe we can look up news articles to see if we can find strange happenings, like Mr. Hofstrom suggested. He did say weird, subtle things were usually

a good sign of a zombie infestation. We would really need to do our research for this," Evie said. She tried not to sound too happy about doing research.

Tiffany nodded before she stood and picked up her tray. "Okay, but what counts as a 'strange happening'?"

Evie brightened. "Well, something wouldn't be in the paper unless it was noteworthy. So I can track that." She grinned. "You know, we should probably start a spreadsheet or something to keep track! That would make a lot of this easier."

Biting into his sandwich, Zach said, "That's a really good idea."

Evie nodded enthusiastically. "I'll take care of it. That way we can cross-reference any strange happenings with where they happened to get a better idea of whether or not the incidents are close together!"

"Hey, good thinking, Evie," Jeff said.

Tiffany grinned. "It really is! This way we can see if this is just a bunch of strange things happening . . .

or a bunch of strange things happening in a pattern.
I'm glad you're on our side, with that super scary brain
of yours." Tiffany waved to all of them. "I have to go.
I have student council right now, but I can search after
lunch during my free period. I'll text if I find anything,
and you can add it to your database, after the quiz show
tryouts."

Tiffany walked off and Evie started poking at her
noodles again, lost in thought. Zach patted her on the
shoulder. "I'm sure you'll get picked tonight."

"What?" Evie said. "I was thinking of the
spreadsheet." She wasn't totally lying.

"Come on, we can tell you're bummed about not
being chosen." Jeff grinned and leaned in close. "I know
how easily you get discouraged when things go wrong.
Relax. Maybe just try to have fun with it and don't
overthink it."

It seemed like everyone was telling her to stop
thinking so much. Evie frowned and didn't say
anything.

Jeff and Zach started talking about a show Zach liked to watch, *Gem War Attack*, and Evie ate the rest of her food as she considered what her brother had said. It wasn't as though Evie didn't know how to have fun, it was just that what she considered fun was learning new things. School was fun, reading was fun. She'd only been interested in the quiz show when she thought it was going to be about answering hard questions. Evie sighed.

Maybe her brother and Ms. Fillman were right. Maybe she should try to have fun the way other kids had fun.

She squared her shoulders. Maybe just this once, she could try to think less about an activity and just do it. If she went with the flow for once, maybe she could be a little more like other kids. It couldn't possibly hurt, could it?

CHAPTER SEVEN
Trying Again

After lunch, Evie's resolve to stop thinking so much weakened. She decided to search for the kids who'd been picked for the show the night before so she could find out why they'd been picked and she hadn't. Were the quiz show people looking for someone funny, or maybe just someone with a quirky personality? Evie knew that people had been chosen for some other reason besides being smart, but she didn't understand what. This was a perfect time for the scientific method, and part of the method was testing out a hypothesis.

Right now the quiz they'd all taken was the only evidence she had to work with.

She needed more.

Mason Briggs was out — that much she knew. But Shelby Brannigan, Adam Paul, and Gerald Bringham were all out as well. None of the kids who'd been picked for the show had made it to school the next day.

It was weird. Weird enough for Evie to tell Tiffany about it on the way to the tryouts after school.

"Wait, so none of them were in school today?" Tiffany asked.

Evie shook her head. "Nope. I asked their friends. None of them came to school."

Tiffany pulled her phone out of her pocket and began texting.

"Who are you texting?" Evie asked.

"Zach and Jeff. This is too coincidental. We need to investigate."

"Did the story about the family with the missing brains check out?" Evie asked.

Tiffany shook her head. "No, I didn't find anything on the Internet about it. Didn't you get my text?"

Evie shook her head. "My phone died. So, the story wasn't true?"

Tiffany shook her head. "No, I found it on one of those spoof sites that takes pictures of people and creates fake news stories as a joke. And it was debunked on another site. So, dead family in the lake? Definitely not real. But this, all four kids at the quiz show tryouts disappearing? It's weird. You know how I feel about weird."

Evie nodded. Tiffany didn't believe in coincidences, and for good reason. Most coincidences in Devils' Pass were monsters cooking up some kind of shenanigans.

Tiffany also didn't like shenanigans, and Evie had to agree with her. There was a scientific principle called Occam's Razor that said the answer that required the fewest assumptions was usually the one that was true. In Devils' Pass that meant monsters. Monsters that ate people.

Anything that led to people getting eaten was not good.

Evie tapped her chin. "Do you think the people hosting the quiz show are monsters? Or zombies in particular?"

Tiffany shrugged. "Maybe. But probably not. I really doubt they're zombies. We don't have the pattern Mr. Hofstrom talked about — no internal organs missing anywhere, nothing super strange . . . except the kids not coming to school today. But that could be any type of monster, if it is even a monster. Still, maybe you can investigate a little during the tryouts tonight, just in case."

Evie's eyes widened. "Me? By myself?"

Tiffany smiled. "You and your brains. I wouldn't want to mess with your brains, personally."

As they walked, Evie thought of the possibility that the quiz show people were zombies. Mr. Hofstrom had said that zombies loved learning, but did that mean they ran a quiz show? It was the perfect job for a zombie since it would let them travel all over pretty easily. Each town could hold new victims.

Evie shivered. The thought of zombies traveling across the country, tricking people so they could eat them, made her feel uneasy. It was bad enough to think they could come to Devils' Pass, but to imagine an entire continent full of monsters? That was very scary. But, if so, someone would have heard of this. The entire country wouldn't have goldfish memory.

Evie discarded the idea. There just wasn't enough evidence to support the idea that the quiz show people were zombies. And more than enough evidence to make it highly unlikely. These were just friendly quiz show producers, trying to make a great show.

When they got to Devils' Pass High School, Tiffany put her hands on Evie's shoulders. "See if you can figure out whether Mason and the rest disappeared from here or later. I can't miss my field hockey clinic. My grandma will be so angry at me for skipping the chance for extra practice. I have to improve my aim or I'm never going to get to play forward this year. If you need me, I'll be in the gym."

Tiffany made her way down the hall and Evie headed to the cafeteria.

Just like the night before, there were a lot of people sitting around and waiting. This time there were no quizzes or worksheets, and Evie sat down at a table in back. Her palms were sweaty. How had Mason and the others gone missing? What kind of monster stalked the citizens of Devils' Pass this time?

The same man from the night before, Hans Gehrin, walked to the front of the room. Tonight he wore a green sweater vest. Was he a monster? He looked so normal. The man wasn't the only adult in the room. There were also a couple of ladies with pale skin and short, brown hair. The women looked enough alike that they could have been sisters. One wore a red sweater vest, and the other a blue one. They each wore knee-length skirts, and they reminded Evie of her elementary school librarian, Mrs. Koonts, who had been eaten last year by a killer rabbit. Evie always felt bad when someone got eaten by an Otherside monster, but Mrs. Koonts had been extra upsetting. She used to order science books just for Evie.

Mrs. Koonts hadn't been a monster, and it didn't seem likely that these people were, either. Evie relaxed. Whatever had grabbed Mason and the other kids must have gotten them after the tryouts when they were on their way home. That didn't sound like zombies. Or at least what she knew of them.

But that meant there could be some cookie elves or killer rabbits or brain toads or doom unicorns or a hundred Otherside monsters they'd faced before stalking Devils' Pass. The thought wasn't much more comforting to Evie.

The man at the front cleared his throat. "Hello, everyone. To those of you who are here for the first time, welcome. Those who were here last night, I'm glad to see we haven't scared you away." He laughed a little, and a few people laughed politely.

"As you can see, tonight I'm joined by a few more of my quiz show associates. And since we have the

extra help, we're going to run things a little differently. Instead of having you answer individual questionnaires, we're going to take folks down the hall to a few of the classrooms in groups of four and interview you that way. If everyone could come to the front and sign up on the sheet, we'll start calling you back."

Evie's hands slicked with sweat. This was completely different! Evie was not a fan of surprises. She walked to the front of the room and signed her name, and by the time she walked back to her table, Zach and Jeff were walking in the cafeteria doors. Jeff had worn his prosthetic leg, but he was walking a little funny, the way he did when it began to bother him.

"I thought you guys weren't coming," Evie said.

"Tiffany texted and said that we had a monster mystery," Jeff said. "So, what's up?"

Quickly, Evie filled him in on why Tiffany had texted. He nodded. "OK, so not zombies. I guess that's good. Why don't Zach and I scout outside to see if there are any clues?"

"Sounds good to me," Zach said.

"But, what am I supposed to do?" Evie asked.

There was a tapping on the microphone as Hans Gehrin approached it once more. "All right, thank you, everyone. Could the following people follow us? Evie Allen, Crystal Ballard, Derek Chase, and Gilda Espinoza?" he called.

Jeff grinned. "Stay here and get on TV!"

Evie stood up and realized she was shaking with excitement. "I can do this. I'm going to do this."

Evie walked toward the room behind the others. Hans Gehrin walked in front of them, a little bounce in his step. Evie almost laughed — he looked like almost every science teacher she'd ever had. And he seemed so . . . bouncy and happy. Something pinged at the back of her mind . . .

She stopped. Hadn't Mr. Hofstrom said zombies looked like normal teachers and coaches? Her hands slicked with sweat again, but this time at the thought of being in a zombie den.

She took a deep breath and shook her head. "You're overthinking things again, Evie," she mumbled to herself. Jeff and everyone else were right. She needed to relax, stop thinking so much, and go with the flow. Not everything was a puzzle to figure out. Not everyone was a monster.

The man stopped down the hall and then spoke to each of the contestants. When it was Evie's turn, he asked, "Evie Allen?" She nodded.

"Go to room twenty-three and they'll begin your interview." The man gave her a wide, happy smile and Evie couldn't help but smile back. She couldn't believe she thought he was a monster just two seconds ago.

"OK," Evie said. "Room twenty-three. Got it." She was nervous, but she wasn't sure if that was because she wanted to be on the show or because she was trying to hard to relax.

There was only one way to find out.

CHAPTER EIGHT

Definitely Not Normal

Room twenty-three was just a normal classroom. There were rows of student desks and a large teacher's desk at the front of the room. The other three kids were already there, and one of the brown-haired ladies stood at the front of the room behind the big teacher's desk, watching them intently. Evie thought she saw a spot of drool fall from the woman's mouth onto the desk.

Evie blinked. Had that really just happened?

She almost giggled to herself. She was overthinking again. Evie closed her eyes, took several deep breaths to clear her mind like she always did before a test, and reopened her eyes.

No more thinking unless it would get her on the show.

"Hello, dear," the woman said when she saw Evie. "Go ahead and take a seat."

Evie found a seat three rows back. Two of the other kids sat in the front row and a girl Evie didn't recognize was in the back row. The girl in the back row had pale skin and short brown hair. In fact, she looked like an exact duplicate of the other two ladies working for the quiz show, just younger.

A prickle of apprehension ran down Evie's spine. Something did not feel right.

She tamped down the feeling. She was overthinking.

"So, the first thing we're going to do is ask you questions about Devils' Pass. Since you all live here, it should be easy for you all to tell me something interesting about your hometown."

Evie sat back and listened as the two kids in the front row eagerly raised their hands and answered questions. The woman asked things like, "Who has the best frozen yogurt here?" and "What is your first memory of the town?" The girl in the back row didn't answer any questions, and Evie was too focused on watching the lady at the front of the room to raise her hand. There was something strange about the woman's mouth whenever she smiled, like her mouth was just a tiny bit too wide.

Evie looked around the classroom, and then out the window. She saw Hans walk by, and she did a double take.

He was carrying what looked like a body wrapped in a sheet.

She sat up straight. Surely she wasn't seeing that right. She squinted and looked harder. The sheet was thrown over his shoulder, and she saw she'd been right: Hans Gehrin was carrying a body wrapped in a sheet.

There was even a dark stain at one end Evie was pretty sure was blood.

Derek Chase noticed the man too, and pointed to the window.

"Hey, what's going on out there?" he asked.

Evie's question exactly.

"Oh, drat. Looks like we're starting early," the older woman said.

Without warning, the woman jumped over the desk and grabbed Derek. The girl in the front row ran to the door, struggling with the knob before opening it and running down the hallway, screaming. For a long moment Evie couldn't process what she was seeing.

And then it all hit her: the quiz show people were monsters.

Turned out, she wasn't overthinking it.

Evie grabbed the arm of the girl in the back row and pulled her to the door.

"What are you doing?" the girl asked, pulling back.

"Come on, we have to get out of here," she said.

The girl laughed, her jaw unhinging like a snake's would, making her mouth huge. "I'm not going anywhere. I'm going to enjoy your delicious brain meats."

Evie reeled and stepped back. They weren't just any monsters. It looked like there were zombies in Devils' Pass after all.

Evie dodged the girl and leapt over the desk, grabbing the trash can near the door and using it to whack the zombie in the face. As she fell to the floor, Evie ran toward the zombie woman, who now had Derek's entire head in her mouth, as though she were going to swallow him whole. Derek flailed about, but wasn't doing much but tiring himself out.

Evie dropped the trash can and grabbed Derek around the waist, pulling quickly. His head came out of the zombie woman's mouth with a wet popping sound. The zombie woman fell backwards, tripping over a desk chair and hitting the floor with a thump. Derek looked around the room with a dazed expression, his face covered in saliva.

"Run!" Evie said, pushing Derek toward the door.

The zombie woman stood and opened her mouth impossibly wide, her extra-long tongue lolling out of the side. She vaulted the desks, bounding toward Evie — but Evie was already moving toward the door. She kicked a desk backward at the zombie lady, tripping the creature up. In front of her, Derek shoved the younger zombie girl roughly to the side. It was just enough for Evie and Derek to dash out into the hall.

"Run, run!' Evie yelled again as they sprinted down the hallway. As she ran, a thought repeated in her head: going with the flow wasn't all it was cracked up to be. In fact, at that moment, Evie was really grateful for her overthinking brain.

"My mom told me I wasn't ever supposed to hit a girl," Derek said.

"That wasn't a girl, that was a monster! They tried to eat you!"

Derek frowned as he ran, and then yawned widely. "I'm so tired," he said, and then suddenly tried to lie down in the middle of the hallway. Evie tripped and quickly scrambled to her feet. She yanked hard on Derek's arm.

"No, no, no, no sleeping!" she yelled. It had to be the saliva all over his face. Mr. Hofstrom said that zombie saliva had a narcotic effect. Derek was going to end up asleep right where the zombies could find him. Evie had to get him out of the school before he ended up getting eaten.

"Jeff! Zach! Tiffany! Help!" she screamed as she ran toward the gym, pulling Derek by the hand. At one end of the hallway was the cafeteria and at the other were a couple of doors that looked like they led to the gym. Evie waited a moment before deciding to sprint toward the ones that most likely led to the field hockey clinic, dragging Derek down the slippery hallway. He was still walking, but just barely.

Tiffany would know what to do.

Evie burst through the doors into the gym, but it was completely empty. There were field hockey sticks scattered around the floor and a dark puddle of what looked like blood. Evie thought she saw streaks of blood on the walls too.

It looked bad, really bad. Where was Tiffany? Had something bad happened to her?

Derek tried to sit down, and Evie had to keep pulling on his arm to keep him moving. He'd stopped talking and had started snoring softly.

Evie ran across the gym, Derek following as she pulled him along, and scooped up a field hockey stick as she ran. It probably wouldn't be much use against a ravenous zombie, but it was better than nothing. She had to keep Derek safe until he woke up.

Evie ran all the way across the gym and to the doors on the far side. They were locked. The sound of running feet behind her caused Evie to drop Derek's hand and whirl around. Derek fell to the ground and started snoring loudly.

"Silly, silly girl. Thought you were so smart. Your smarts will make your brain meat that much more delicious," the older lady zombie said. She stood in the doorway that led back to the main hallway. Her mouth opened impossibly wide, and Evie could see that she had no teeth, just lips like a snake would have. It was the scariest thing she'd ever seen. Evie froze. How was she supposed to fight back against that? With just a hockey stick?

But a thought struck her: she had more than a hockey stick. She had her delicious, overthinking brain. And she had friends.

A side door burst open, slamming into Derek's body. Tiffany stuck her head around the edge of the door. "In here!"

Evie didn't hesitate. "Take his hand," she said. Tiffany grabbed Derek's hand and pulled while Evie pushed on his legs, trying to get his dead weight through the door.

The older lady zombie ran toward the locker room doors. She moved faster than Evie could push Derek, so Evie did a quick calculation and changed her plan, moving to intercept the zombie.

"Tiffany, get Derek! I'll take care of the zombie," Evie said as she skidded to a stop in front of the zombie lady. The monster grinned and dropped into a crouch.

"So smart. So delicious. Not at all like that boy we ate last night. Much better," the zombie said, her long tongue hanging out of the side of her mouth, dripping saliva.

"What boy?" Evie demanded.

"Who cares who? Two others too. Not very tasty. We're all still so hungry," the zombie lady said. And then she leapt at Evie.

Evie sidestepped the lunging zombie woman and used the hockey stick to trip her. The creature went down with a thump, and Evie turned and ran to the locker room, colliding with Tiffany and Derek just inside the door.

Tiffany let go of Derek, reached around Evie, and slammed the door shut. She grabbed a cricket bat from a nearby bucket of sports equipment and used it to secure the handle.

"Tiffany! I'm so happy to see you." She gave Tiffany a huge hug. "It appears there are, in fact, zombies in the high school." Then she burst into nervous giggles. "I mean, in case you missed the lady with the huge mouth trying to eat Derek and me."

"Uh, yeah," Tiffany said. She pointed to a woman lying on the floor, her eyes wide as she stared at the ceiling. It took a long moment for Evie to realize that part of the woman's head was missing, her skull empty.

Someone had eaten her brain.

"Who is that?" Evie asked, taking a step back.

"My field hockey coach. Luckily I managed to get the rest of the girls to safety before they also ended up as dinner." Tiffany wrapped her arms around herself and sniffled a bit. "I hate these stupid monsters."

Evie wrapped her arms around Tiffany and hugged her again. "At least you got the rest of the girls to safety. We just have to figure out what to do next." Now that they were safe for a moment, Evie was starting to worry.

"Speaking of getting people to safety, Evie, good job with Derek. Anyone else probably would have left him behind and saved themselves." Tiffany pointed to the floor where Derek snored loudly. He was completely out.

"Have you heard from Jeff or Zach?" Evie asked. She felt dizzy and a bit weird, but she knew that was just her brain trying to panic. Zombies were serious business, and it would be nice to get hysterical and freak out about it all. But that wouldn't be helpful.

Tiffany shook her head. "I don't know. They aren't answering my text messages. But I do know one thing."

Evie gripped her field hockey stick. "And what is that?"

"We are in deep, deep doo-doo."

CHAPTER NINE

Bottoms Up!

Seeing the blood in pools around the locker room made Evie lightheaded. But she took a deep breath and then she and Tiffany grabbed Derek. Each of them took one of his arms and led him to a locker and locked him in. He was too heavy to keep dragging through the school, and they hoped that when he woke up, the zombie emergency would be over.

After Derek was taken care of, Tiffany and Evie moved to the locker room office. Once they were settled, Evie quickly outlined what had happened since Tiffany had dropped her off at the quiz show tryouts. Tiffany nodded as Evie talked, and when Evie got to the part about the man carrying a body wrapped in a sheet, Tiffany stopped her.

"Wait, why are the zombies taking the bodies? They already ate the brains."

"Maybe they need other parts of the body as well?" Evie offered. "Mr. Hofstrom said that there are all kind of zombies, and that some eat hearts or livers or whatever."

"Hmm. If that's the case, they'll be coming back for the body in the locker room," Tiffany said.

Right at that moment, there was a banging on the locker room door, and both Evie and Tiffany jumped. The locker room door shook and the cricket bat cracked as someone tried to shove the door open. As they watched through the window, the cricket bat began to give way.

"We have to keep moving," Tiffany said, picking up

her hockey stick and gesturing for Evie to pick up hers. "Until we know how to beat the zombies the only thing we can do is try to get out of the school. Maybe Mr. Hofstrom can keep us safe."

"Do you think we'll be able to beat them?" Evie asked.

Tiffany shrugged, but Evie could tell from her wide eyes that Tiffany was just as scared as she was. They always knew how to beat the monsters that came from the Otherside. Not having a plan was terrifying.

They quietly opened the back office door and made their way to a main hallway. It was eerily silent in the hall, nothing at all like the zombie movies Evie had seen with her brother. In those, people were screaming as they ran and the zombies sounded like growling monsters. Here, the only noise was the slight squeak of their tennis shoes on the hallway tiles. The doors at either end of the hallway were dark, and the sickly yellow glow of the overhead lights cast shadows everywhere. One of the lights flickered suddenly and Evie jumped, nearly dropping her field hockey stick.

"Look. There's a light coming from that classroom." Tiffany pointed down the hallway.

"We should go the opposite way," Evie said.

Tiffany nodded. "Agreed."

They cut down a hallway and found themselves in a dead end. The only thing that was at the end of a hallway was a science room.

Tiffany tried the door, and it opened easily. They slid in, and once they were inside, Tiffany gestured to the teacher's desk.

"Help me push it in front of the door," she said.

The desk squeaked and groaned as they pushed, and Evie's heart pounded. There was no way the zombies hadn't heard them.

"We're don't have much time. They're going to come to see what that noise was," she said, wiping sweat from her temple.

Tiffany nodded. "I know. Let's brainstorm what we know about Otherside monsters to figure out how to beat these zombies. We need Evie Allen super smarts."

Evie paced as she began to think. "Well, we know from experience Otherside monsters are usually destroyed by regular things in our world. Fire and water, mirrors, hot sauce. We should try one of the things that have worked before to see if we can use that to defeat them, starting with the easiest things to find. Like water or a mirror somewhere," Evie concluded.

Tiffany's phone pinged, and she looked at it. "It's from Zach and Jeff. They're hiding out in the cafeteria kitchen. They said the zombies started attacking people a few minutes ago. A lot of people got out of the building, but a few people didn't make it."

"Do they have any idea how to defeat the zombies?" Evie asked while Tiffany responded on her phone.

Tiffany shook her head. "They said, 'We were hoping you had figured that out.' I'm going to tell them your theory about using something that worked before. Since they're in the cafeteria, maybe they can start gathering ingredients to try on one of the zombies."

Evie's eyes widened. "That sounds like a terrible plan."

Tiffany grimaced. "I know. But terrible is pretty much all we've got."

Evie walked around the room while Tiffany texted back and forth with the boys. The high school science room was way cooler than the science room at the middle school. There were Bunsen burners and a huge saltwater aquarium in the one corner, with clownfish, coral, and a blue tang. Evie loved fish, and as she moved closer to take a look, but a noise came from the back of the room — a loud scraping sound as if someone had pushed a desk out of the way.

Tiffany looked up from her phone and said, "Uh-oh." The door at the back of the classroom crashed open and two zombies, the girl zombie and the older lady zombie, ran into the room, laughing in delight as though they'd just won a prize.

"Run!" Tiffany yelled.

"Where?" Evie yelled back. The only door was the one blocked by the desk. And there were two drooling, big-mouthed monsters between them and it.

Tiffany swung her hockey stick, tripping the older lady zombie. "Good point! OK, we fight!"

Evie looked around, panicked. Her eyes trained on the saltwater fish tank.

Water. That had worked on other monsters.

There was a plastic cup next to the fish tank, so Evie flipped open the top of the tank and dipped the cup in. She flung water at the girl zombie, just as she lunged toward her.

The water hit her full in the face. Tiffany backpedaled down the aisle until she stood next to Evie, the girl zombie coming closer with slow, deliberate steps.

"OK, so water isn't their weakness," Tiffany said.

"Yes it is! Look!" Evie pointed at the zombie. Her face was starting to melt, her features slowly dripping down. She let out a wounded howl.

"We need more water," Tiffany said, her eyes wide and hopeful.

Evie reached into the tank and got another cupful

of water. She threw it at the shriveling zombie. She and Tiffany watched as the monster shriveled up like a melting slug.

"I can't believe the water works!" Tiffany said.

"Tiffany, watch out!" Evie yelled. The second zombie had regained her feet and came vaulting over the lab tables at Tiffany.

Tiffany raised her hockey stick, but it was too late. The zombie grabbed her by the waist and ran from the room before Evie could do anything more than scream.

The melting zombie began to make noises that sounded like "glub glub glub," but Evie ignored it. Instead she ran out into the hallway, desperate to save her friend.

But there was no sign of Tiffany, anywhere.

CHAPTER TEN

Outside Interests

The hallways were still eerily quiet as Evie made her way to the cafeteria. She ran as fast as she could even though she couldn't seem to stop crying. Tears fell down her face, and she sniffed. She had to be strong. She would find Zach and Jeff, and they would all save Tiffany.

They had to.

Evie noticed that it was after eight p.m. when she sprinted past a hallway clock. Was her mom worrying about her right now? Or had goldfish memory kicked in and already erased Evie from her mind? Evie always wondered how that worked, how families could just forget about how the people they loved fell victim to Otherside monsters. What did they think had happened to them? Sickness? Or maybe they just assumed they'd left and were living somewhere else?

Evie quickly found the cafeteria and slid into the room. Just as with the gym, there were smears and splatters of blood on the walls, and a couple of kids Evie knew from the middle school lay on the floor, their bodies bent in strange angles.

Evie made sure not to look at them for too long.

"You made it!" Jeff yelled as he and Zach came running out of the cafeteria.

"Tiffany didn't," Evie said. "We have to find her. We figured out water beats the zombies, so we just need some water bottles and we should be able to—"

"Look out!" Zach yelled, cutting Evie off. She spun around to see two zombies, both of them small like her, standing in the doorway.

"How many zombies are there?" Jeff asked.

"Too many," Evie said, following the boys as they turned and ran to the kitchen.

The sound of the zombie laughter turned Evie's blood cold. How could they save Tiffany when there were so many zombies and they didn't even know where she was?

They made their way to the kitchen at the back of the cafeteria and slammed the door shut. The zombie kids hit the door, trying to get in, but the door was heavy and made of metal. Even so, Zach, Jeff, and Evie all leaned with their backs against the door. Each time the zombies hit it, her bones rattled.

"So, water, huh?" Jeff asked.

Evie nodded. Jeff ran to get a bottle of water from the package on a shelf and then he stood a few feet away.

"OK, open the door," Jeff said, crouching.

The zombies slammed into the door and Zach shook his head.

"Are you serious?" Zach asked. "No way we're going to let those monsters in!"

"If you don't start melting some of these zombies, we're never going to be able to find Tiffany," he said. "So, let's start melting some zombies!"

The monsters slammed into the door once more and Evie stood a little bit behind her brother. "Jeff is right. We have to stop running and start fighting. Otherwise, what will happen to Tiffany?"

Zach sighed, and turned around to grab the door handle. "Are you sure?"

Jeff nodded and twisted the cap off of the water, throwing it to the side.

"Count of three," Zach said. "One, two—"

On the count of three, Zach pulled the metal door wide. One of the zombies ran into the room.

"Oh, no you don't, you creep," Jeff said, as he flung the water at the zombie's face.

The zombie just stood there, watching him, looking a little irritated that he had water on his face.

Then he leapt.

"It didn't work," Jeff yelped as the zombie tackled him. Jeff scurried away, grabbing onions off a low shelf and pelting the zombie with them as he tried to escape. The other zombie ran into the room and Zach tripped him, causing him to crash into the zombie trying to eat Jeff.

While all of this was happening, Evie's brain ran through the calculations. She replayed what had happened in the science room in her mind. Tiffany had been in trouble, and Evie had gotten a cup and dipped it into the fish tank before throwing it at the zombie …

"Salt!" Evie yelled. "The water we used was from a saltwater tank! It must be the salt that made them melt."

Evie ran toward the shelf that contained flour and other dry goods and grabbed a blue container of salt. She pried off the lid and threw a handful of salt at the nearest zombie. The salt stuck to his skin and he howled as he began to melt.

"Oh, super gross!' Zach yelled, jumping to get away from the rapidly spreading puddle of zombie goo. He ran over to Jeff and helped him climb to his feet.

The other zombie, seeing the salt, tried to run.

"Grab him! He might know where Tiffany is!" Evie yelled.

Jeff sprinted after the zombie and tackled him from behind. The zombie opened his mouth and tried to lick Jeff.

"Don't let him lick you or you'll fall asleep!" Evie yelled, jumping over the puddle of zombie goo and running toward her brother. Zach followed closely behind.

Jeff jumped off of the zombie, but not before Evie stood there over the monster, salt in one hand. "Tell me where you took my friend."

The monster started to leap at Evie, and she shook the salt threateningly.

"I'm never telling you," he said, his voice whispery, like a snake slithering through leaves.

The zombie lunged for Evie, and she dumped the salt container over its head. In a matter of seconds, the zombie was just a puddle of slime.

Evie sighed. "So, salt melts them — that's great. But we have about who knows how many to melt and we have to do it quickly before they eat Tiffany. Anyone have any ideas where to start?"

Zach and Jeff looked at each other and shrugged.

Evie crossed her arms. "OK, then let's split up and melt as many zombies as we can. Keep your eyes out for clues and see if you can't get one of them to talk!"

Jeff's and Zach's pockets began to beep, and they took their phones out and looked at them in surprise. "It's a text from Tiffany," Zach said.

"What? What does she say?" Evie asked.

Zach read the text out loud. "She says, 'A zombie put me in the back of a tractor trailer behind the school with a bunch of other kids. Hurry.'"

Evie's expression turned hard and determined. "There's no time to waste. Let's go," Evie said, running toward the shelf and the other containers of salt.

As she started to open the containers, Evie thought her science teacher Ms. Fillman had been completely wrong.

She had lots of outside interests. And one of them was saving people.

By using her brain.

CHAPTER ELEVEN
Goo Is Gross

They emptied the boxes of salt into the boys'
pockets. Because she didn't have any pockets in her
skirt, Evie emptied hers into a backpack she had found.
When they all were loaded up, Evie led the way out of
the cafeteria to the back of the school. The hallways
were still empty, but they weren't quiet any more, since
they were filled with the sound of the Loyal Order of
Helga heading out to save the day.

Evie was not a fast runner, and she didn't
particularly like sprinting, but as they made their way

through the halls and to the parking lot, she was pretty sure she set a speed record. Once they were outside, the cold hit Evie like ice water in the face. It stole her breath and surprised her, but she pushed the discomfort aside.

She had to save her friend.

Evie ran across the snowy grass to the parking lot where the truck full of people stood. The truck was easy to see, bright white, the kind of tractor trailer that shipped fruits and vegetables. But the big rear doors were still open, and there, trying to escape the dozen or so zombies pushing people into the truck, was Tiffany, looking completely unharmed. Unharmed but not happy.

The zombies saw Zach, Jeff, and Evie approaching and ran to intercept them, jaws hanging open like they were going to swallow the Loyal Order of Helga whole. A couple of zombies lurched toward Evie, and she threw handfuls of salt at them as she ran past. It was only the howls she heard as they started to melt that let her know she'd actually hit them.

A zombie rose up before her. Evie flung a handful of salt at her. The salt hit the zombie full in the face and she started to melt, pained howls coming from her throat as she fell apart.

Evie didn't wait for the zombie to become a puddle. She was already moving to the next zombie, jogging across the parking lot and flinging handfuls of salt as much as she could. Some of the salt got in her eyes and made them burn, but she didn't have time to do much besides rub them with the back of her hand before moving on to the next monster. There was another ten yards to the truck, but the parking lot was packed with zombies. It felt like Evie would never make it the short distance to the truck, but then, somehow, she was there.

The zombie closing the back end of the tractor trailer tried to run away as Evie got closer, but she was faster. She chased him toward the edge of the parking lot and a single handful of salt was all that was necessary to end the creeper.

"You can't stop us," a gravelly voice said from behind Evie. She turned around and there a trio of older zombie women stood, their brown hair and gaping mouths making them difficult to tell apart.

"We already have," Evie said.

The old women laughed. "You think so? Devils' Pass was just the first town. Soon, people all over the country are going to be trying out for quiz shows, and we'll be there to take their delicious brain meats."

"Maybe," said Evie, "but I'm willing to bet there will be kids just like us at every single tryout with a pocket full of salt to take you down." Evie flung a handful of salt at the zombie closest to her. She howled in pain while the other two lunged for Evie.

Evie tripped and fell as one grabbed her foot. She wedged her hand in her bag and managed to throw another handful of salt into the monster's face. Evie scrambled backward from the zombies and ran into someone. Strong arms wrapped around her middle.

"I got you!" the zombie said.

"Not quite," Evie said, tossing a handful of salt over her head at the zombie holding her. The monster screamed and let her go. Just before the monster melted, Evie got a glimpse of the man in charge of the quiz show tryouts — Hans Gehrin, a zombie after all — his nose falling down his face and melting into a puddle of goo.

She looked around. No more zombies. Just gross puddles of goo melting into the ground.

"I'm going to have nightmares for weeks," she muttered. But she breathed a huge sigh of relief.

"Yep. Total nightmares here," said Jeff, walking up beside her. "Seriously. Why do the monsters always have to be so gross? Can't we get monsters that just disappear cleanly, once?"

Evie nodded. "I know. Let's check on Tiffany."

"Zach's got her," Jeff said, pointing to where Zach was helping Tiffany stand.

"What about everyone else in the tractor trailer?" Evie asked.

"I think they're going to be fine," Jeff said, pointing to the truck.

The people in the back of the truck were starting to wake up, and there were sirens sounding far off and getting closer to the school.

"Come on, that's our signal to get out of here," Jeff said.

"First, I have to do something," Evie said, and walked fast into the school.

She ran through the hallways and to the locker room. She found a pair of bolt cutters in the coach's office and snipped off the lock that kept the locker Derek was in shut. He blinked sleepily at Evie. "Did I fall asleep in here?" he asked.

Evie helped him up. "Something like that," she said. She grinned as she led him outside to the crowd.

The Loyal Order of Helga began walking home from Devils' Pass High School. A drowsy Tiffany balanced between Jeff and Zach, yawning widely. Evie's stomach growled.

"Sorry," she said. "I missed dinner."

"I cannot believe you're hungry," said Jeff.

Tiffany stirred, shaking off some the effects of the zombie saliva. "Did someone mention food?" she asked, her voice slow and sleepy.

Everyone laughed. Things were back to normal.

CHAPTER THIRTEEN

Um...Other Othersides?

The next day at school, people weren't talking about the zombies who had eaten people's brains and had tried to kidnap a bunch of other people. Instead, people were talking about the bus accident that had killed a bunch of people, including the high school field hockey coach. No one was completely sure where the accident had happened or how, but there was a nice flower memorial at the front of the school and a card for people to sign.

Evie stared out over the cafeteria and sighed. "I will never get used to that."

"Goldfish memory?" Tiffany said. She shrugged. "I don't know, it's better than everyone knowing that we're totally heroes."

"You'd probably get your lunch for free if everyone knew we were heroes," Zach said.

"You'd definitely get seconds," Jeff said, sliding the remainder of his tater tot casserole across the table to Tiffany.

"OK, but then who would eat your leftovers?" Tiffany said, winking at Jeff.

There was a pinging noise and Tiffany pulled out her phone. She stared at her phone for a long time before frowning.

"Who is it?" Evie asked.

"Mr. Hofstrom. I stopped by the library this morning to tell him about the salt so he could add it to his book. He didn't answer so I wrote him a note and slid it into the book return as well as texting him."

"Did you also tell him what they said to Evie about Devils' Pass being the first town?" Jeff asked.

Tiffany nodded. "Yeah, I told him all of that."

"Oh, that's a good idea," Evie said. "So, why do you look so upset?"

"Because, his text message says, 'Good work. I'll let the other librarians in the other towns know so they can be on the lookout for the zombies.'"

Zach sputtered on his chocolate milk, coughing and choking. "Wait, what? 'Other librarians?' 'Other towns'?"

Tiffany, Evie, Jeff, and Zach all looked at each other.

Evie said slowly, "There are other towns like Devils' Pass?"

That meant there were other places where kids fought monsters to keep their towns safe. Other portals to the Otherside.

And maybe, other monsters they'd never even heard of.

Yet.

Evie pushed her avocado sandwich away. "I think I just lost my appetite," she whispered. "How come we've never heard of these other towns and librarians?"

Tiffany frowned. "What if we have and just don't remember? What if the Loyal Order of Helga has its own kind of goldfish memory? The LOH magic is weird. What if we weren't allowed to remember there are other towns like Devils' Pass until now?"

Zach pushed his hand through his hair. "What, you mean like we've leveled up somehow after figuring out how to beat the zombies on our own?"

Jeff nodded, understanding dawning across his face. "That makes sense."

"And that means beating the monsters is only going to get harder," Zach said.

They all fell silent.

It looked like their lives in Devils' Pass were about to get even more interesting.

DO NOT ATTEMPT TO READ IT OR YOU WILL SUFFER ACUTE GOLDFISH MEMORY.

A SAMPLING OF OTHERSIDE MONSTERS, IN ALPHABETICAL ORDER BY SPECIES

Aardvarks, ghost: pig-like creatures with no physical body that likes to live in the trees. Aardvarks on Earth are burrow dwellers and like to dig. Otherside aardvarks climb trees, die, and become ghosts. They feed off brain energy and by possessing people as they come close. They prefer pitch black and forests with mist. Can be defeated with a quartz stone bathed in moonlight and shone on them as they sit in the trees.

Albatross: large sea birds, usually found near bodies of water. Hangs around the necks of people filled with regret, eventually weighing them down so much that they can no longer move. Can be easily defeated by convincing the victim of the albatross to give the people they wronged a heartfelt apology.

Basilisks, Bug: large insect-like creatures with a shiny black body, six legs, and one hundred antennae. Each antenna contains an eyeball of a different color. One look from a basilisk can turn a person to stone, and basilisk sightings can be common in gardens and resort areas in Otherside towns. Basilisks are drawn to beautiful landscaping, and are especially partial to flowers. People turned to stone by a basilisk's stare can be cured with a misting of rose water. Pregnant basilisks are especially aggressive, and are easily identified by the clutch of bright pink eggs on their backs. Do not confront a pregnant basilisk.

Brain Toads: prefer moist, woodland locations but will also quickly adapt to life in an urban setting by hiding in bathrooms. Appear as bright red with white spots. When attached to a host, brain toads can appear as a fedora or baseball cap, but will reveal their true nature when doused with water. Brain toads feed on the brainwaves of their host, eventually killing the host as the host loses the ability to reason. They can be destroyed by quizzing the host on state capitals or math problems such as multiplication tables. This will overload the brain toad and it will explode. Mr. Hofstrom's note: warn folks about the very sticky, very stinky properties of the exploding toads. Everyone involved will smell like sardines and onions for a week.

Chupacabras: part goat, part sheep, part lizard, chupacabras are common in the southern United States. They are known to feed on cattle and other livestock, swallowing them whole and leaving behind nothing but a pile of bones. Chupacabras love music, especially music with a quick beat, and they can be trapped by playing it at top volume. Once trapped, chupacabras can be fed a tin can, after which they will turn into a regular, harmless goat. More a nuisance species than anything to fear, chupacabras are also known for their beautiful pelts and in the olden days trappers would make coats ou,t of them. Chupacabra hunting is now illegal, and the head librarian should be contacted if chupacabra hunting is suspected.

Clowns: although not all clowns are Otherside monsters, many are. Clowns can be found in sewer drains and circuses, and prey on the fear and tears of small children. They can be defeated by being told in a calm and direct voice, "You aren't funny." If that doesn't work shoot them in the face with plain seltzer.

Dragons: appearing at first as small, yet friendly lizards, at puberty these creatures grow to house-size proportions. Dragons are intelligent but uninterested in humans, mostly, unless there is not another source of food nearby. To defeat them, place puzzles and brainteasers near the portal to the Otherside and they will gather them up and disappear to work on them on their own.

Dream Wraiths: like Nightmares, Dream Wraiths cause terrible dream-visions when their victims fall asleep. However, a Dream Wraith only appears as a ghostly person with tattered clothes and dark holes for eyes. Dream Wraiths are former humans who have become spirits after being trapped in the Otherside — they find their victims to become human again. To do so, they must terrorize their victims until their will to live is over and then the Dream Wraiths inhabit their bodies. To vanquish them, find out what human they used to be and tell them stories about their lives. They will disappear and move on.

Elves, Cake: usually found in bakeries and small towns. They can occasionally be found in a forest clearing. Cake elves are between sixteen and twenty-four inches tall with mottled gray skin that appears damp, similar to a frog's. These creatures spin their mossy hair into delicious confections which are highly addictive to their prey. Elves are elemental creatures, and can only be destroyed by the opposite of their elemental properties. Fire can be destroyed with water and vice versa. Earth elves can be destroyed with a strong wind, and air cake elves have only been encountered on the Otherside, where they float on clouds and throw cakes onto their unsuspecting prey.

ELVES, COOKIE

Origin: *Otherside*

Colors: *gray, multi-color hair*

Likes: *eating humans; cookies; minions*

Dislikes: *Water. Water will defeat them.*

Note on hair: Their hair can be molded into anything. It gives off an odor and taste pleasing to humans.

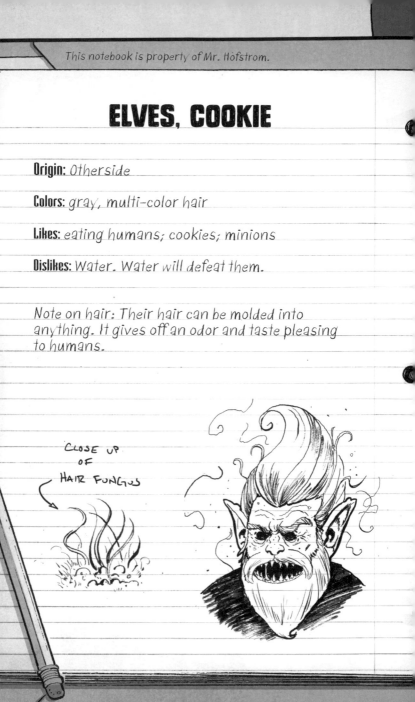

CLOSE UP
OF
HAIR FUNGUS

This creature is usually found in bakeries, especially in small towns. Cookie elves are between sixteen and twenty four inches tall with mottled gray, bumpy skin similar to a toad's. These creatures have hair that is made of a fungus that resembles dryer lint. They spin their hair into cookies to lure in their victims.

Unlike cake elves, cookie elves often use their prey as mindless servants prior to eating them. They can also be destroyed by using the opposite of their element.

Note: encountered cookie elves, were destroyed with water. Believe that these cookies elves did not come through the sinkhole in Devils' Pass. Reach out to other librarians to see if they have also seen these elves.

HATES
FIRE
&
WATER

H^2O

Elves, Holiday: they do not exist with the exception of those at the North Pole. Very industrious, always wear green or red velvet attire. Do not engage holiday elves without consulting with the head librarian.

Faeries: prefer grassy areas. They appear as small, bug-like creatures no longer than an inch long and are known for leaving very itchy bites. Not usually a significant threat unless led to swarm by a queen. Faerie queens are slightly larger than regular faeries and sparkle in the sunlight. All faeries feed on sunshine, and they will reproduce and become more numerous the more light they consume. Swarming faeries can clog the area, stealing the sunlight and killing crops and trees. Faeries can be destroyed with a 1:2 solution of lemon juice and water.

Gargoyles: found only in large cities. Appear to be stone during the day and gain a giant part-bat, part-man aspect at night. Lives off of human food and not considered a threat to humans. Gargoyles have been known to protect large cities from Otherside creatures. If encountered, contact the head librarian.

Giants, Earth: Earth Giants are often mistaken by people for hills or landslides. In fact, Earth Giants are large creatures made entirely of mud. They are easily defeated by a strong rain or a garden hose. Unlike Ice Giants and Fire Giants, Earth Giants do not feed on humans. They can be best defeated by asking them nicely to lie down and become hills.

Giant, Ice: Ice Giants are made entirely of snow and ice and they live entirely on eating humans. Unlike fire and Earth Giants, Ice Giants enjoy eating people and spitting out their bones. These creatures can be defeated with a flaming torch or other source of open flame. Ice Giants are only a serious problem in winter.

Giants, Fire: Fire Giants are made entirely of flame and tower above most humans. They prefer to stalk woodlands, and many people mistake them for forest fires. Though humans are not their first food source, they often eat them in the course of eating woodlands. They can be subdued with a large amount of water.

Gorgons: found in areas with a large number of children. Gorgons can appear as tall men or women and are known for their beautiful hair. They are friendly to humans and can discipline children who misbehave by turning them to stone with their gaze until they choose to release them. Gorgons make excellent teachers and are vegetarians. If encountered, log their presence with the head librarian.

Griffins: half-eagle, half-lion creatures that hunts and feeds on Elves. Griffins prefer open spaces and have been sighted near sphinx prides in desert regions. Griffins often leave remnants of their meals near their lairs to warn off other creatures. Griffins are extremely dangerous if encountered, but can be easily lured to sleep by singing them a lullaby. The tune "Rock a bye Baby" seems to be the most preferred song.

Harpies: beautiful birds with the head of a woman. Harpies tend to hide in bushes and wait for people to pass. Once a person is within earshot, they yell encouraging messages like, "YOU GOT THIS!" and, "YOU CAN DO IT! KEEP TRYING!" It's customary to reward such responses with walnuts or pecans, which Harpies love. Harpies also make lovely pets, and will appear as regular parrots to anyone unable to see or remember Otherside monsters.

Hippogriffs: half-eagle, half-horse creatures known for having several magical properties. Most remaining hippogriffs Earth-side are miniature versions of the original hippogriffs that stalk the Otherside and are the size of a large dog. Usually found on the tops of buildings near gargoyles. Hippogriffs are friendly, intelligent, and make excellent pets, but require large quantities of fish. They have been known to be extremely useful in organizing information and shelving books.

Librarians wishing to keep hippogriffs as pets are required to get clearance from the head librarian.

Jackalopes: a part-rabbit, part-antelope creatures that feeds on hair. Usually found in close proximity to hair salons, where they can find an endless array of hair clippings. Jackalopes are docile creatures that prefer to avoid all human contact, but if confronted they will charge with their antlers. Keep jackalopes away from large cities and towns with hair offerings left out in clearings.

Manticores: lion creatures with a scorpion's tail and the face of a woman. Manticores feed on humans, eating them in a single gulp. Although they have no specific habitat, manticores have been found to congregate near schools, as they prefer to eat children over full-grown adults. Their scorpion-like tails are used to subdue prey before they ingest them. Manticores can be defeated with handfuls of candy or a spray of soda. They are very sensitive to sugar. Note: clear, lemon-lime sodas seem to be more effective than colas.

Mermaids, Freshwater: usually live in stagnant, slow moving water such as ponds and roadside ditches. They appear as beautiful women with greenish, scale-covered skin and long, algae-covered hair, and they have very, very sharp claws instead of hands. They also have sharp-pointed teeth, and a lot of them. Freshwater Mermaids feed on mammals, and have been shown to have a fondness for cats and small dogs, as well as some humans. They can best be destroyed by being left to dry out in the sun. Lure them out of their water hideouts with stinky cheese such as Limburger or smoked gouda. Once completely dried out, they will transform to frogs and are completely harmless.

Mermaids, Saltwater: live in the ocean and brackish inland locations. Like Freshwater Mermaids, they appear as beautiful women with scale-covered skin. Saltwater Mermaids have long strands of kelp for hair and very sharp teeth in addition to their claws. They prefer to feed on people, most especially surfers, and many "shark attacks" are in actuality Saltwater Mermaid attacks. They have been shown to prefer strawberry smoothies, and once lured out of the water and completely dried out, will turn into harmless piles of kelp and sea foam.

Nightmares: Nightmares are similar to dream wraiths, but can take many forms in the victims' dreams. Nightmares inflict terrifying dream-visions on their victims and cause them to sleepwalk out of cities — they prefer their victims near farms and barns. When the victims' fear has peaked, the Nightmares become black smoke and then solidify into unicorn-shaped darkness, and eat the person they've targeted. Nightmares can be easily defeated once in unicorn form by distracting them with coffee, then dousing them with warm milk or, on some occasions, chamomile tea. Note: the Nightmare's victim must be asleep before the Nightmare will appear. Defeating these creatures is definitely a team effort.

Rage bees: these creatures look just like regular bees, but appear in a swarm to punish people who are guilty of being mean to others. The first case of rage bees was spotted outside of a Chicago suburb, where a young girl was being teased and her bullies were viciously attacked. These creatures appear to be a mutation of an Otherside honey bee. Rage bees are best vanquished, if needed, through the use of kind words and lots of chocolate cake.

Red Dogs: large, ghostly, rust-colored dogs that stalk highways and country roads, especially in the fall. Red Dogs will appear suddenly in the hopes of startling drivers off the road where they will then consume their life forces. Most Red Dogs spend their time in a normal dog form. Red Dogs can be defeated with squeaky toys, which will trap them in their normal form and rob them of their hunger for human souls.

UNICORNS

Origin: *Otherside*

Colors: *white body; golden horn; pink, blue, multicolor manes*

Likes: *apples, humans, large meadows, places to graze, lullabies, moving in herds*

Dislikes: *hot sauce, being made visible, being hungry*

Note on teeth: Unicorns have three rows of sharp, pointed teeth on their upper and lower jaws.

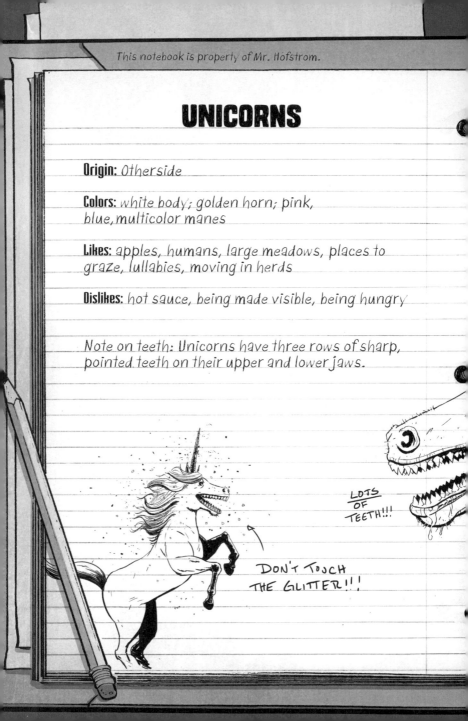

LOTS OF TEETH!!!

DON'T TOUCH THE GLITTER!!!

This creature prefers grassy meadows and sparse woodlands. Unicorns feed exclusively on humans, most especially humans who are under exceptional amounts of stress. The beautiful, rainbow-hued manes of unicorns shed a metallic substance that looks like normal craft store glitter and immediately sends susceptible folks into a blissful state. Unicorns have several rows of very sharp teeth similar to a shark's. Unicorns are also one of the few monsters able to travel between the Otherside and the real world with ease.

They have been known to use their horns to stab those who are not subdued. Unicorns are invisible until their hooves get wet. When in the Otherside unicorns can be best avoided by wearing a necklace of peppers from the pickle pepper plant. Mr. Hofstrom's note: unicorns can be destroyed by a liberal application of hot sauce. Be warned that this leaves behind a very large pile of glitter (useful for sphinxes — don't forget to collect).

PEPPERS?

VAMPIRES

Origin: *Otherside*

Colors: *appear as beautiful humans, but when revealed in a mirror, are hideous monsters*

Likes: *all types of energy — physical, emotional, mental. Love creating situations that allow for continuous feeding*

Dislikes: *mirrors; free thought; disobedience; smart humans*

Note: minions will attack when trapped

Creatures that feed on human emotions rather than blood, vampires often appear as beautiful men and women with an amazing sense of fashion. They feed on their human victims as well as controlling their minds. The vampires can control any human it has fed from, no matter how recent the feeding. Vampires have a hive mentality, in that lesser vampires work for a lead vampire known as a king or queen. The only proven way to see a vampire's true form or destroy them is with a mirror. By forcing a vampire to look into the mirror they are forced to realize that they are truly a monster and will spontaneously combust.

Note: some vampires have taken to using modern technology to hunt their victims. Watch for addiction to TV shows, phone applications, and online games to find the vampire victims. The only way to cure the victims is to destroy the king or queen.

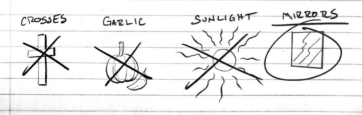

CROSSES   GARLIC   SUNLIGHT   MIRRORS

ZOMBIES

Origin: *Otherside*

Colors: *appear as humans, but when hungry they, are hideous monsters*

Likes: *all types of energy — physical, emotional, mental. Love creating situations that allow for continuous feeding*

Dislikes: *salt; people who aren't smart; losing*

Note: zombies are extremely dangerous and cunning. They have destroyed entire towns.

GIANT MOUTHS!!

There are several known varieties of zombies, the most popular being kidney zombies, which feed on the kidneys of unsuspecting tourists. Zombies are a very clever group of creatures, as diverse in their methods as they are in their diet. They appear as completely normal people, and contain venomous saliva that incapacitates their victims shortly after contact. There is currently no definitive way to defeat zombies, but any librarian who encounters these terrifying creatures should notify other librarians as soon as possible. Zombies tend to spread rapidly.

Note: encountered brain zombies running a quiz show, destroyed with salt. Update sent to librarian network with a copy to the head librarian in Saint Paul, MN.

GLOSSARY

apprehensive–to feel nervous or uneasy

carnivorous–a plant or animal that eats other animals

flail–to wave or swing arms and legs all around

foreboding–a sense that something isn`t right

narcotic–a substance to make a person feel drugged, or sleepy

pore–to go over something in a very focused way

scientific method–seeing a problem; collecting data about the problem; and checking it through tests and experiments to see if the understanding of it is correct

shenanigans–tricks or nonsense

shrivel–to shrink because of lack of moisture

vault–to jump over something

YOU SHOULD TALK

1. Throughout the story, people kept telling Evie to stop thinking so much. Do you think they were right? Would she have been able to save the day if she hadn't thought things through?

2. What made the zombies particularly hard for the Loyal Order of Helga to defeat?

3. The LOH finds out there are other towns that have Otherside problems. What do you think this means for the future of the Order?

WRITE ON

1. Write a letter from Ms. Fillman to Evie explaining how she thinks Evie should find different activities to engage in. Now, write how Evie would respond after defeating the zombies.

2. If you were a quiz show zombie, what would you write on a flyer to make sure people came to try out? Pretend you are a zombie and make a flyer that appeals to middle school students and would talk them into trying out.

3. Pretend you are Evie reaching out to another kid in a different town that deals with Otherside monsters. What questions would you ask? Write an email to the other monster hunter whom you don't know.

ABOUT THE AUTHOR

Justina Ireland lives with her husband, kid, and dog in Pennsylvania. She is the author of *Vengeance Bound* and *Promise of Shadows*, both from Simon and Schuster Books for Young Readers. Her forthcoming young adult book *Dread Nation* will be available in 2018 from HarperCollins and her adult debut *The Never and the Now* will be available from Tor/Macmillan. You can find Justina on Twitter as @justinaireland or visit her website, justinaireland.com.

ABOUT THE ILLUSTRATOR

Tyler Champion is a freelance illustrator and designer. He grew up in Kentucky before moving to New Jersey to develop his passion at The Joe Kubert School of Cartoon and Graphic Art. After graduating in 2010 he headed back south to Nashville, Tennessee, where he currently resides with his girlfriend and soon to be first kiddo. He has produced work for magazines, comics, design companies, and now children's books; including work for Sony Music, F(r)iction magazine, Paradigm Games, and Tell-A-Graphics. You can see more of his work at tylerchampionart.com.